DATE DUE

APR 2 2 2004			

PREPOSTEROUS FABLES
FOR UNUSUAL CHILDREN

The Tooth Fairy

The Maestro

The Wolf King

The Sorcerer's Last Words

THE
SORCERER'S
LAST WORDS

Written and illustrated
by Judd Palmer

BAYEUX

Special thanks to the folks who helped to make this book possible: Ashis Gupta, Dave Lane, Jenny Lane, Jim Palmer, Steve Pearce.

THE SORCERER'S LAST WORDS
© 2003 Judd Palmer and Bayeux Arts, Inc.
Published by: Bayeux Arts, Inc., 119 Stratton Crescent SW, Calgary, Canada T3H 1T7 www.bayeux.com

Cover design by David Lane & Judd Palmer
Typography and book design by David Lane
Edited by Jennifer Mattern

National Library of Canada Cataloguing in Publication
Palmer, Judd, 1972-
       The sorcerer's last words / Judd Palmer ; illustrations
        by the author.
       (Preposterous fables for unusual children)
       ISBN 1-896209-84-X
    I. Title. II. Series: Palmer, Judd, 1972- Preposterous fables
    for unusual children.
PS8581.A555S67 2003   jC813'.6   C2003-905354-7

First Printing: September 2003
Printed in Canada

The Publisher gratefully acknowledges the financial support of the Canada Council for the Arts, the Alberta Foundation for the Arts, and the Government of Canada through The Book Publishing Industry Development Program.

to the Old Trouts

"The transcendent world is therefore open to him that has sufficient Will to triumph over the forces that guard it; but woe to that man who approaches it with a passionate and selfish heart; with lowered head he will fall back into the current of decomposition, where he will be dissolved. Nature destroys all Evil; it is the law of selection!"

—*Initiation*, Francois Charles Bartlet, 1889

Und sie laufen! Naß und nässer

Wirds im Saal und auf den Stufen:

Welch entsetzliches Gewässer!

Herr und Meister, hör mich rufen!

Deep and deeper grows the water

On the stairs and in the hall,

Rushing in with roar and clatter—

Lord and master, hear me call!

—*Der Zauberlehrling*, Johann Wolfgang von
Goethe, 1779: *The Sorcerer's Apprentice*, translation
by W.E. Aytoun and T. Martin, 1859

O. The Apprentice

THE WATER: SUBSIDES.

What once was torrent, now is trickle; deluge is now drip; flood, a fwip, plip, plink, plop; and then, silence.

The apprentice lies sprawled, soggy, near death.

"Let this be a lesson to you, Humboldt," says the Sorcerer. "A sorcerer seeks wisdom, not power."

And Humboldt, who has learned his lesson indeed, believes him with all his heart.

He feels a prickling on the back of his neck, and twists his head to see what lurks behind him. In the corner rests the Broom, unsplintered, not even wet. Humboldt shudders and looks at his master.

His master is gone.

In the Sorcerer's Library was a book which Humboldt was strictly forbidden to touch. It was locked behind a door on the top shelf of the bookcase, and it was always guarded by an enormous owl. The key to the lock hung at all times around the Sorcerer's neck.

Humboldt was the Sorcerer's Apprentice. He had lived in the castle ever since he was a small boy, and he knew little of the outside world except that in it was no greater wizard than his master.

Humboldt thought that, since he was his master's apprentice, he would learn mighty enchantments and one day become as great and powerful as the Sorcerer. But the Sorcerer never taught him anything.

Instead, Humboldt did chores. He had a thousand crushing duties, but most arduous was the filling of the Aquarium. Each day he was required to carry bucket after bucket of water from the well up a thousand stairs, back down, buckets empty, back up, buckets full, back down, buckets empty, back up, buckets full, and on and on. Each night he fell into his bed cursing, for he knew his master could fill the Aquarium with the merest twitch of his powers.

And one day, his master left the castle to go to a meeting of wizards. Humboldt was alone. While cleaning the Library, he discovered the key. Whether his master had forgotten it in his hurry or had left it by design, Humboldt did not know, but he had cause to ruminate on the subject a great deal in the years that followed.

The Owl was asleep, a miracle. Humboldt crept up the ladder and inserted the key. The door opened and there lay the Book of Books. He leafed through its pages, comprehending nothing, until he found a passage he could understand: Broom Magic.

He uttered the secret words and sure enough, the Broom in the corner shivered and then sprang to attention. Humboldt was delighted. He ordered it to pick up the cursed bucket and to descend the cursed stairs, then fill the bucket with water, climb back up the stairs, and pour the water into the Aquarium. The Broom obeyed.

Humboldt spent his day lounging like a king while the Broom filled and poured, filled and poured. He did not notice when the Aquarium began to overflow.

But he did notice when the water began to

pour into the Library. Humboldt was horrified; the carpets were soaked and many books were ruined. He commanded the Broom to stop.

But the Broom did not stop. Humboldt did not know the right incantation, or the Broom's awakened will was stronger than Humboldt could control. The Broom continued to fill and pour, fill and pour, and the castle's halls ran with flowing water up to Humboldt's ankles.

There was no recourse but the axe. In a fury of shame and hatred, Humboldt chopped the sinister Broom into splinters.

But the splinters sprang into action, skittering down the halls like a scattering swarm of rats. Humboldt splashed after them, frantically swinging the axe, but the splinters were obscenely fast, and Humboldt could not catch them. He watched with dread as the splinters returned from below carrying yet more buckets like gleeful pallbearers, chattering amongst each other.

The torrent rose and Humboldt was engulfed. His mouth was filled with waves, and his legs flailed against the swirling currents. He thrashed and gulped for air as the world itself was swallowed in the flood and darkness.

Underwater the cosmos slowed and Humboldt felt a dreadful peace. He saw his arms moving and felt his lungs bulge in his chest, but it no longer mattered to him. A strange gold light filled his mind, obliterating all his memories. The water felt warm. He tried to formulate his last thoughts, but he found he knew no words. All that remained was the steady throb of an enormous heart which he didn't think was his own. And then he didn't even know what difference there might be if it were his heart or not: Humboldt's heart, or the heart of the world? He could not remember who Humboldt was. He was about to die.

But then came the voice of the Sorcerer:

THE APPRENTICE

HE WHO DROWNS
BE NOW UNDROWNED
WATER NOW UNPOUR
ALL THAT'S DONE BE NOW UNDONE
BROOM BE BROOM ONCE MORE

I. The Sorcerer

THE SORCERER DOES NOT LEAVE the Library anymore.

In the old days, the Sorcerer was always turning up in unexpected places. Humboldt would be feeding the beasts and suddenly realize the Sorcerer was watching him from the shadows above, perched on a rafter. Or Humboldt would discover him behind a tapestry he was dusting, or peering through a crack in the floorboards, his faintly luminescent eyes flickering to follow him. Sometimes the Sorcerer would be climbing out of the Aquarium, his ferocious black eyebrows plastered wet on his forehead, and Humboldt would run and fetch a towel. It seemed to Humboldt that, in those days, the Sorcerer took a kind of pleasure in moving around, or perhaps in investigating the corners and crannies of the castle. But as the Sorcerer grew old, his travels grew rarer and rarer, and each time he appeared he was paler and more wrinkled. His eyebrows turned white; sometimes they would be all Humboldt could see, fluttering about in the shadows like the ghosts of two ravens. The last time the Sorcerer appeared he was crouched by the well, muttering, his back curved like a pensive vulture, his skin dry and translucent like a frosted window.

That was several years ago. Now, Humboldt moves through the castle feeling quite alone.

On the Library door is posted Humboldt's

list of chores. The list has never changed, as far as Humboldt can remember, but he is required to check it every day. It is his first duty, to receive his orders, which are written in an ancient ink that has turned brown and smudged on yellow parchment. The letters are neat and tiny, and Humboldt would need to squint if he ever bothered to read them. But he knows them by rote now. He repeats the list to himself like an incantation, rocking back and forth on his heels and twiddling his thumbs. He listens as he murmurs for any sign of the Sorcerer behind the door, but there is no sound except the occasional rustle of the Owl flapping about.

But he knows the Sorcerer is there, because he is not anywhere else, and the rest of the castle is Humboldt's domain.

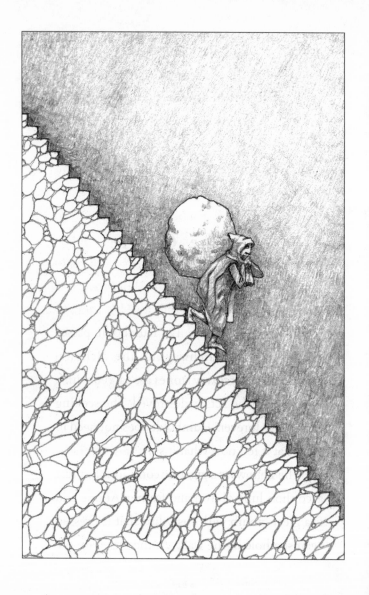

II. The Castle

CHORE NUMBER 12: Humboldt passes under the archway to the Bellows-Chamber. The archway stones are carved with a motto: "He who acts is destroyed. The seeking Mind lives forever." Humboldt does not need to glance at it to know what it says.

The Bellows is a gigantic contraption, a vast accordion lung of iron and leather. At one end is a great mouth with rusty lips that is pressed against a hole in the wall. At the other are the baffles, which draw air from outside to clear the castle dankness that has collected overnight.

From its nozzle extend a hundred corroded pipes which carry the air along walls and through floors and ceilings to the endless chambers of the castle. It is too huge to be operated by hand; the great baffles could only be compressed by a giant.

Humboldt must climb a ladder to stand on the baffle-lever, holding a collection of lead weights so that he is heavy enough to budge it. As the baffle-lever lowers there is a slow and enormous wheeze like a mountain exhaling. The old leather creaks, and elsewhere in the castle the air stirs faintly. Humboldt races back up the ladder as the Bellows inhales and the lever rises, and then he clambers back on to push it down again. After a few times, there is a soft breeze in the corridors and halls, and the Bellows heaves and rasps of its own accord, the asthmatic breathing of the castle.

Chore number 54: Humboldt has his shoes off, his trousers rolled up, and his cloak gathered about his waist. He is in the Garden, and he likes the feeling of dirt between his toes.

The Garden is still and dark. Humboldt feels his way in the shadows with a lantern strapped to his head, groping in the soil. His stomach always rumbles at this time of day.

He has a basket, and he is filling it with mushrooms, which grow in the dark. There are no windows in the castle, no sunlight to make a vegetable grow. If Humboldt had ever tasted an onion or a tomato he would be tired of mushrooms, but he has not, and so he takes great pleasure in their musty smell as he plucks their little pale bodies from their warm burrows. He turns them in his fingers, feeling their pleasing plumpness, and then drops them in his basket.

Sometimes he talks affectionately to the mushrooms. He likes their quiet self-assurance, but he knows he mustn't get too attached to any mushroom in particular, because, after all, he is going to eat them. There was a mushroom once that Humboldt particularly liked, and he kept it next to his bed so they could while away the night hours together. But the mushroom soon grew black and wrinkly, and Humboldt felt guilty. Perhaps the mushroom was lonely, or didn't feel the same way about Humboldt. Finally, Humboldt ate it for a midnight snack. Now, when he is lonely at night, he just goes and sits in the Garden, pleased to know that he has a thousand quiet friends, sitting like little bald gnomes meditating peacefully in the dark.

Chore number 79: Humboldt trudges through the Bestiary, collecting spittle from the birdcages. He doesn't like the racket.

Chore number 127: Humboldt hates the Pit. It is excruciatingly hot. He needs to take off his cloak and hang it by the entrance. Then he picks up the garbage sack again and pushes the heavy door open with his shoulder.

There is a blast of stench and fire on his face. He squints and tries to breathe through his mouth, although he doesn't like the thought of the stink on his tongue.

He staggers under the weight of the sack towards the furnace, which sits like a great fat black iron toad in the bottom of the Pit. Its mouth is agape with flame, casting a flickering glow on Humboldt's sweating brow as he labours down the staircase which winds around the sloping walls.

There are rats that live down there, feeding on the slops that dribble from the furnace's chin. They are evil and hairless, their flesh singed, and they squeak to each other and scamper on their blackened toes to gather around Humboldt's feet as he makes his way to the bottom. He heaves the contents of the sack into the furnace maw, shaking the last bits out, and then, unburdened, runs back up the stairs to escape.

Chore number 168: Humboldt mops Wilhelm's room while Wilhelm presses his great oily body into the corner, twitching the end of his tail with agitation.

Chore number 214: Humboldt reads a story to the Blatherwump until it appears to be asleep.

Chore number 342: Humboldt polishes the beakers, misting them with his breath and then wiping them with a cloth, careful not to disturb the contents, which have fragile tempers.

Chore number 596: Humboldt is getting quite tired, but he takes a deep breath and continues. Wisdom is patience, he thinks.

III. The Well

I N THE VERY DEEPEST PART of the castle is the Well. Humboldt plods down the stairs, empty buckets swinging. The steps are furrowed and smoothed by ten thousand trudges.

As he descends, the walls grow black with damp trickles in the cracks, moss encroaching with a deep and living green. Humboldt's fingers trail over the wall, balancing him on the slippery stone, and his fingertips come away stained and slightly stinky. By the time he

reaches the bottom everything is completely covered by the moss, a strange vegetable architecture.

Great pillars disappear into the dripping dark. The ponderous weight of the castle is above, all the spires and halls and floors resting on the arches and beams of the Well chamber. The atmosphere is dank and heavy.

The water is like a black mirror. Humboldt's reflection is grimly still, and it does not ripple when he dips his buckets. Beneath the surface are the world's deeps.

He hauls the buckets back up the stairs, his shoulders hunched, his knees trembling a little with each step. He is always glad to leave the Well behind him, because water makes him nervous, and the depthlessness of that place is dreadful.

Finally he reaches the Aquarium. He tips the buckets on the edge, and the water pours thickly down the hole. It makes a kind of gulping noise when it hits bottom.

Humboldt doesn't know where all the water goes every day, only that the Aquarium needs constant refilling. He thinks there might be something down there swallowing the water, but it is too murky to tell. He used to wonder about it a great deal, to occupy his mind as he heaved the slopping buckets up the stairs, but no matter how much he pondered he never got any closer to an answer. Now he just plods and pours, plods and pours, never wondering about anything.

"Take him, Sorcerer," Humboldt's father had said. "Give him a better life. I can only offer him hard, unending labour, and I would be so happy to see him get along a little better."

Humboldt was frightened of the Sorcerer, who stood at the doorway to their hut, filling the frame like a man peering into a gopher hole. The Sorcerer grinned, attempting to be welcoming, but to Humboldt he was leering like a hungry ghoul. The Sorcerer extended his arms.

"Go with him, Humboldt," said his father. "A poor man's life is toil." He hefted Humboldt like a bundle of sticks and handed him to the frightening man.

The Sorcerer gathered Humboldt in his arms, and then, with Humboldt pressed against his shoulder, he handed something to Humboldt's father. Humboldt heard the clink of gold coins. He looked out the door over the Sorcerer's shoulder at the trees and hills beyond, and thought to himself, yes. This will be much better. I will become a Sorcerer and never have to be so poor as my father.

The Sorcerer turned, and now Humboldt's home swung into his view. His father stood on the step, calloused, grubby, his shoulders mus-cled and hunched. His father waved, but

Humboldt simply watched as the Sorcerer walked and the little dirty shack with the sign above its door, 'Brume-Makker', grew smaller and smaller until finally, it disappeared.

IV. The Messenger

HUMBOLDT IS ON ONE of the staircases leading along the walls of the lower atrium. By the light of his lantern many other staircases can be glimpsed, spiraling and criss-crossing in the darkness. He can hear the muffled singing of the goats as he approaches their chamber: chore number 47.

Humboldt doesn't hate the chores any-more. It's a habit of mind he's developed. If he thinks about the chores, how many he's done,

how many he's got left, the fact that he'll be doing them all again tomorrow, he festers with resentment and grinds his teeth and the chores take forever. But if he does the right trick with his brain, he finds he can just float away while his body does the work. It's a difficult thing to do. It's taken him years to perfect it. But now he can easily silence his thoughts, almost like he is sleepwalking, and then suddenly realize that his chores are done. He thinks it might be the very thing the Sorcerer is trying to teach him. His mind is slowly changing.

Sometimes a thought will creep into his head without his noticing, and he'll find himself thinking about how steep the stairs are, or how much his shoulders hurt, or how many more buckets he needs to fetch. Very quickly those thoughts turn to resentment, and the resentment makes him think of the Broom, and how the Broom could do all the chores if the Sorcerer just said a few words.

Before Humboldt knows it, he hates the Sorcerer. Wisdom is getting somebody else to do what you don't feel like doing, he thinks, that's all.

But then he remembers the horror of the flood, the water in his lungs, the terrible silence under the surface. And he realizes how his thoughts have deceived him again.

He recites his chores to clear his mind of evil. He finds it somehow comforting, the rhythm and repetition. He doesn't think about the chores, just repeats the inexorable numbers and instructions, and soon he is thinking of nothing at all.

And so he has a completely empty head when he opens the door to the Goat Room. And this chore is particularly arduous: he must sweep, and to sweep he needs the Broom. It takes extraordinary peace of mind for him to touch the handle, to overcome the menace he feels vibrating in its wooden sinews, the way it seems to whisper awful things as it rustles along the stones.

He makes his way through the bustling and bumping throng, the Broom held over his head. The goats are singing very beautifully today. Their heads are lifted up, their eyes closed as they shuffle about in their traditional dance, their lips moving with the words. The goatsong is long; Humboldt notes that they are only through the first movement, in which the Great Goat is first prophesied to be king. They are coming to a part with very complicated harmonies, and they are paying very little attention to Humboldt.

All is as it should be. Humboldt feels content. But when he turns he sees the Owl in the doorway.

The Owl is very large; it is hunched to peer through the door frame. It is difficult to make out any emotion in its unblinking eyes. Its beak is cruelly curved so that it always looks like it is frowning. But now it looks agitated. It is shift-ing from foot to foot anxiously.

Humboldt is confused. The Owl guards the Book. It never leaves its post. It seems like it has come to summon Humboldt. Or maybe to warn him.

The Owl heaves its wings and is gone. Humboldt comes to the door and looks out. He catches a glimpse of the white feathers, lumi-nescent in the dark as the Owl glides out of sight. It is headed towards the Library.

Humboldt decides to follow. Perhaps some-thing is wrong. Perhaps the Sorcerer needs him. Humboldt's composure is teetering. He must go knock on the door.

V. The Book

HUMBOLDT ARRIVES at the Library door. It is closed. The chore list flutters a little in the castle breeze, but otherwise all is still and quiet. Now that he is here, he is too nervous to knock. He is not to disturb the Sorcerer for any reason.

Humboldt fidgets with his sleeve. He presses his ear against the door and listens. Nothing. What if the Sorcerer is ill? What if he is dead? What if he has been dead all these

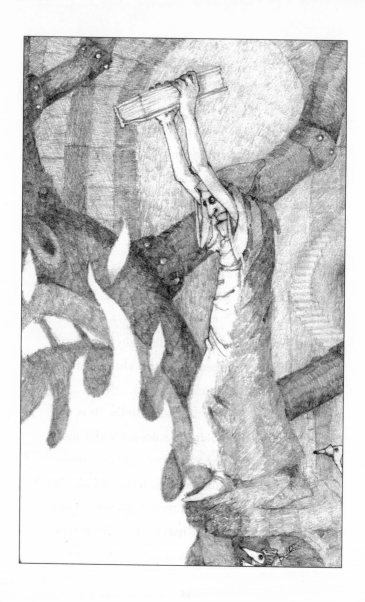

years? It has never occurred to Humboldt. His stomach is in turmoil.

He almost falls over when the door opens. The Sorcerer is standing in front of him.

"Ah, Humboldt. Excellent. It's funny you should come knocking. I happen to need you."

Humboldt nods. He sees that the Sorcerer is holding the Book.

"Take this, Humboldt," says the Sorcerer, presenting the Book. "Take it to the Pit and destroy it."

Humboldt is aghast. He takes the Book with automatic obedience, and clutches it to his chest. He stammers. "Master. . . ?"

The Sorcerer regards him kindly. "It is not your fault, Humboldt. The Book should have been destroyed long ago. I know it was a temptation to you, and when I left yesterday I should have known you would attempt to use it. Because it is in our natures to want power. But we must be vigilant against this desire. It brings only woe, as you now know. A wise man accepts the world as it is; only then can he be happy. Burn the Book."

The Sorcerer recedes into the Library. He leaves the door open.

Humboldt stands with the Book for a while but the Sorcerer does not reappear.

Finally, he heads off down the hall. The Book is heavier than two full buckets, and his arms tremble with its weight.

He stands in the Pit. The ember rats chatter amongst themselves excitedly. The mouth of the furnace glows and a ghastly light flickers on Humboldt's face. Far away the Bellows wheezes and a harsh hot wind blows. The flames leap and Humboldt squints.

He runs back up the stairs with tears blurring his vision. He buries the Book in the garden.

VI. The Dream

WHEN HUMBOLDT DREAMS, he dreams of winter. Perfect, cold, the trees cut into the white sky like etchings in glass, and the shadows on the snow like furrows in a dead man's brow. There is no sound and no wind. There are no footprints in the frosted world, and the ground is no different from the heavens.

And then, a dry rustle. A clack and a snap. Suddenly, Humboldt is aware that he is present

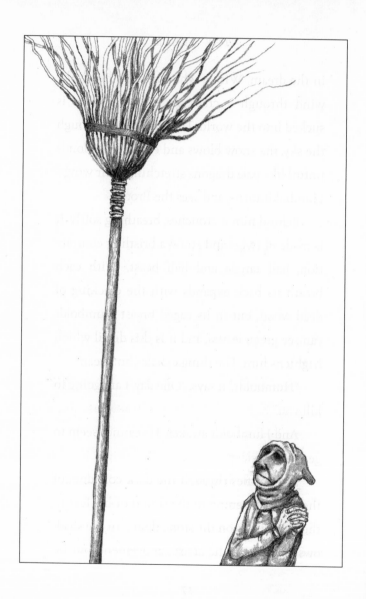

in the dream. With a whoosh and a howl like wind through a crack in the wall, time is sucked into the world. The sun moves through the sky, the snow blows and eddies, the clouds unfurl like pale dragons stretching their wings. Humboldt turns, and sees the Broom.

Behind him it crouches, breathing softly. It is made of twigs and straw, a bristling contraption, half tangle and half beast. With each breath its back expands with the cracking of dead wood, but in its caged breast Humboldt can see green leaves, and it is this detail which frightens him. The thing exhales hot steam.

"Humboldt," it says. "One day, I am going to kill you."

And Humboldt awakes. He cannot seem to get back to sleep.

He shuffles through the dark corridors of the castle, listening to the sound of his feet in their stockings on the stone floors. In the shadows he believes he senses movement, but he knows the castle is still, is stillness itself. He is the only thing that moves.

He comes to the Library. The door is open. There is a dim light behind a pile of books, and Humboldt creeps toward it. There is the Sorcerer, sitting as still as the winter dream, not even breathing. Before him sits a toad in a jar.

The toad is transfixed by the Sorcerer's frozen gaze, the old man's eyes glimmering with a faintly unnatural light. His eyebrows are now so thin that the wrinkled flesh of his brow is visible beneath. The corners of his mouth are slightly wet, but his hands are dry as tree bark. He is part phantom.

The Sorcerer inhales, and his eyes snap from the toad, who breathes a croak of relief and stretches his legs. The Sorcerer regards Humboldt, who stands timidly in the shadows.

"I, too, no longer sleep," says the Sorcerer.

Humboldt nods. He becomes aware of the clock, which has begun to tick, and suddenly he is very tired. The Sorcerer returns to his contemplation, and Humboldt pads quietly back to his dark room. He recites his chores until he falls asleep.

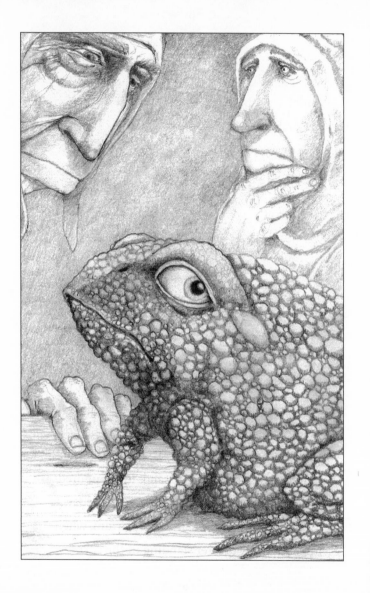

VII. Gold

HUMBOLDT HAS A BUCKET in each hand. They are full of water from the Well, and his arms are tired, but he feels the serenity of ritual in his muscles. He has climbed the steep steps from the deeps, and carried the buckets through the door. They are the four-hundred-and-forty-seventh and four-hundred-and-forty-eighth buckets he has carried today.

He has just arrived at the Aquarium, when he senses the Sorcerer standing in the corner.

"We shall have a guest tomorrow, Humboldt," says the Sorcerer.

Humboldt puts down the buckets. He tries to control his surprise and anxiety. There have never been any guests at the castle. As long as he can remember, there has only ever been the Sorcerer and his beasts.

The Sorcerer's eyes are piercing. "Come to the Library, Humboldt. I have something to show you."

Humboldt follows the Sorcerer through the dark halls to the Library. The Sorcerer seats himself before the jar with the toad, and motions with frail fingers for Humboldt to sit next to him.

Humboldt sits and his belly churns.

"Witness this toad, Humboldt," says the Sorcerer. "Tell me what you see."

Humboldt looks at the toad. It is shiny and looks like a large green wart. The toad puffs its gullet and returns his gaze, its eyes glazed with slime. "I see a toad, Master."

"Yes. Good. That is the beginning. Have you ever heard of alchemy, Humboldt?"

"Indeed I have, Master. It is the science of transforming base things into gold."

"You are right. Many people have spent their lives in its trance. It would be an astonishing power, would it not, to turn something worthless into something so very valuable as gold?"

"It would," says Humboldt.

"But for all the dusty centuries of labour and philosophy, no one has ever succeeded. Why? Because they have never truly understood the cosmos."

"What did they not understand, Master?"

"They sought to use their powers to transform. They did not understand that the toad is already gold. From the perspective of eternity, Humboldt, all things are one thing. Take, for instance, this toad: if I ate this toad, it would soon be merely toad parts in my belly; the juices of my intestines would make those toad parts smaller still, until they could be used by the spirits of my body to make parts of me. The toad's foot, for instance, would become part of my heart, and the toad's tongue would become part of my brain. What once was green and sticky would become a place where I keep my memory—it would become a memory itself, the memory, for example, of how I tie my shoes, or what it was like to play in the river as a little boy with a straw hat and grass-stains on my knees. Do you see?"

"I think so, Master."

"And so: if I die, as surely I will, and I am buried in the ground, as I would like to be, and the centuries pass and the winds blow and the sea heaves, and mountains grow where once there was my grave, what remains of my body will be pushed deeper and deeper into the earth by the rocks piling above.

Finally, my body is consumed in the fires in the centre of the earth, and the tremendous heat makes me into rock, and the tremendous pressure makes that rock very dense, and then mercury and alabaster are mixed with the rock that once was me, and then there is an earthquake, and I am thrust into the air by a volcano, and mixed with the rays of the sun and struck by lightning, which is how gold is made in the earth by the spirits of the underworld, then my body has become gold. Ten thousand years from now, a man is walking along and finds a nugget of gold, and it once was me. Yes?"

"Yes," says Humboldt, squinting a little.

"And thus: The toad is me, and I am gold. His present form is an illusion. In reality, he is both Toad and Gold."

The toad burps.

"It is only a matter of understanding, Humboldt. For the Mind is eternal, and can see things for what they are because it is not bound to Time. Watch."

The Sorcerer observes the toad. He takes a breath, and his eyes flutter shut. His mouth murmurs strange syllables, and his hands make an arcane pattern over the jar. The toad blinks.

The Sorcerer opens his eyes and looks at the toad. Humboldt looks at it as well.

"You see, Humboldt? Here is gold."

Humboldt clears his throat uncomfortably. It is still a toad, as far as he can see.

"Now," the Sorcerer says, repeating the motions of his hands, "it is me."

"I see." Humboldt lies.

"Now, it is a toad."

"That much I can say for sure, Master."

The Sorcerer smiles. "Indeed. That is the true alchemy. Now, if you please, finish your chores."

"Yes, Master Sorcerer," says Humboldt. He

leaves the Library with a great deal to ponder, he thinks to himself.

It is night, and Humboldt dreams again of the Monster.

VIII. The King

HUMBOLDT IS COLLECTING mushrooms when he hears the knocking, a slow and deep pounding in the dark. Humboldt drops the basket, mushrooms tumbling, and runs to let the visitor in. The knocking grows more and more violent as he careens through the halls and stairways until finally he arrives at the gates, panting.

He lifts the great iron latch and pulls the heavy doors open. Sunlight pours into the shadows, and Humboldt blinks. Before him stands something he has not seen since he was a boy: a man from beyond the castle.

The man is huge. He wears purple robes lined with fur, over armour. At his belt hangs a sword. His face, far above tiny Humboldt, is bearded with black bristles, and his eyes are black as well. His brow is deeply scarred, and upon it sits a battered golden crown.

Behind him stand several other men who are also clad in steel. They wear helmets that cover their faces, the eye-slits dark and expressionless. In their gauntletted hands they hold axes.

The man in the crown looks down at Humboldt. He snorts and spits on the ground, and then speaks.

"Sorcerer."

Humboldt feels a shiver. "This way, sir."

"King," says the man.

"I apologize," says Humboldt. "This way, King, sir. Your Highness."

Humboldt turns aside and shows the way. The King strides forward, followed by his knights.

Beneath the cold clank of their armour, Humboldt thinks he hears the rustle of straw.

IX. Death

Humboldt brings the king and his men to the Library. He knocks on the door, and says, "Master, the visitors are here."

"Let them enter," comes the quiet voice of the Sorcerer.

Humboldt holds open the door, and the King and his men walk through it. As Humboldt closes the door, he sees the Sorcerer, old and fragile, sitting at the table. Before him is the toad. The Sorcerer's hands are clasped in front of him.

Humboldt stands outside the Library, anxious, waiting. He can hear the murmur of the Sorcerer speaking.

Muffled through the door, the King's voice bellows. "Gold! Not toad!"

The Sorcerer's voice continues, with a little more urgency. Humboldt cannot hear what he is saying.

The King's voice shouts again. "Gold! Not toad!"

There is a smash, and the Sorcerer shrieks. Humboldt does not know what to do. He throws open the door, and what he sees is a nightmare.

The jar is on the floor, broken. The toad hops around on the floor, until the iron boot of a soldier comes down with a horrible squishing sound. The soldier barks metallic laughter. The King holds the Sorcerer by the throat.

The Sorcerer is quaking; his feet are off the floor and kicking. His lips are moving fast, his eyes darting with panic. The King snorts and spits, glaring at the Sorcerer.

"This knife is a knife," he growls, "not gold. Not toad. Knife."

And with an awful flicker he has a knife in his hand, and then the knife is in the Sorcerer's belly. The Sorcerer coughs and stops his incantation. The King lets him fall to the ground. Humboldt screams.

A soldier cuffs him in the teeth with the handle of his axe, and Humboldt staggers over the table, knocking books everywhere. He finds he cannot get up from where he has fallen; his vision is blurry. But he hears the King.

"Burn," says the King.

Humboldt hears the crash of the lanterns smashing, and the horrible whoosh of burning oil spilling on the stone floor. He moans and rolls from the table. His face hurts badly, and he feels a sudden scorching pain as his leg brushes a crackling stack of burning books. Flames spiral around him as he crawls towards the Sorcerer.

The Sorcerer is sprawled on the floor, his legs twisted under him in a strange way. His face is pale, and there is blood on his lips. There is a dark pool slowly spreading under him. His face contorts, and his eyes dart at Humboldt.

"Humboldt, my son," he whispers. "Come to me."

Humboldt cradles the Sorcerer's white head. Around him the bookshelves burn, and the air is filled with black smoke.

"Let me tell you something, Humboldt. Is there time?" says the Sorcerer. Humboldt sobs while he nods. He will not leave the Sorcerer's side.

"In the end, I think I would have preferred power to wisdom."

And the Sorcerer dies.

X. Fire

HUMBOLDT STAGGERS THROUGH the fire, the castle groaning with its own destruction. The once shadowed halls are now bright, the dank places are now hot. Everywhere the flames are changing things into blowing ash and shrieking embers.

Humboldt is coughing, blind with smoke, as he crashes through the door to the Garden. It is horribly alight with ten thousand burning mushrooms, like candles in a cathedral. The

soil flickers with the awful glow. He is on his knees, digging with his fingers. Past him run the panicked goats, knocking and jostling, and he hears the Blatherwump howling below. He can't save any of them.

He has the Book in his arms and he is running. He falls down the stairs and keeps running. Through the corridors, past the boiling Aquarium. The flagstones are hot through his shoes. Past the Bellows, frantically pumping; past the Bestiary; past the door to the Pit which bursts open belching fire. Out the gates. To the river.

Humboldt splashes into the cold water, clutching the Book to his chest, and turns to watch.

The Sorcerer's castle gives a terrible wail of beams cracking and stones smashing, and then collapses in a glittering spray of sparks. Humboldt's face is smeared with tears and ash, and the river eddies around his bruised knees.

XI. The Tree

THE SUN IS SHINING gently. Wisps of cloud like the breath of grandmothers hang in the sky, which is deeply blue. The forest softly rustles in the breeze, the leaves flickering gold in the light. The river flashes clear and cool over wet rocks.

The world is beautiful. An old rabbit hops along amongst the tree roots, feeling young. It sees a dewy leaf and brushes its nose against it, just like it did when it was small and wide-eyed and full of longing to know everything, like how a dewy leaf feels against one's nose. It feels good.

Humboldt watches the old rabbit with a plume of black smoke in his heart. It is nothing to him but fur and bone and flesh. It annoys him that it is nearby. Stupid rabbit, he thinks. You could be destroyed at any moment, but you just hop around sniffing leaves.

He turns back to the Book, his mind dark. His fingers move slowly along the page, his lips moving with words he doesn't understand. But he keeps reading.

Humboldt lives in the hollow of a great oak tree. He does not eat much, just chews on bits of lichen that grow on the bark of his home. He does not sleep much, and when he does, it is sitting up, his jaw on his chest, the Book on his lap.

Weeks go by and Humboldt grows thick with filth, his hair greasy and his body stinky.

His eyes sink into black pits in his callow face, and his lips grow thin. He looks more and more like one of the roots of the tree, grown over with fungus and bramble, immobile except for his flicking eyes and his murmuring lips.

Slowly the arcane geometries begin to clarify. The syllables connect to the numbers, the symbols open their hidden meanings to him. Each new hieroglyph is like a cave mouth blocked by fallen stones, but slowly he heaves aside the rocks, feeling his way through to the inner deeps of understanding. Sometimes he is threatened by a troglodyte and chased back to the surface, uncomprehending. But the next day he finds the secret password, and the guardians of the symbols step aside to let him pass.

The words that made the world become known to him, the language God spoke when He summoned the earth from the darkness. He learns the names of all things, the forgotten names of dragons, of rocks, of trees, of fire. He learns the names and orders of angels, and their places in the halls of heaven. He learns the circles of inferno, and the lords of the cities of the dead. He learns the paths of the stars and the compositions of the planets, which are made of fire and which of water. He learns the ways of mercury and alabaster. He learns the geography of the earth's arteries, the true meanings of old prophecies, the things philosophers think about but don't tell anyone.

And then, one day, he awakes from the trance. He is completely overgrown, and he has to struggle to free himself from the binding roots. He shakes the moss from his beard, and scrapes the dirt from his cheeks, blinking from within dark holes. He stretches his back, creaking, and steps back from his tree. The Book is under his arm.

When first he tries to speak, his mouth makes no sound. His lungs have been still for too long. He goes and gets a sip of water from the river and returns to his spot feeling better.

His words come as whispers. His fingers are weak and stiff, and he moves them awkwardly. He rustles like a pile of strange leaves, his fingers twitching and his cracked lips moving.

The sun goes down and still he stands reciting, rocking back and forth on his heels like he used to when he read his chores.

The sun comes back up and he is still whispering.

And then, slowly, the old oak tree begins to smoulder. Humboldt grows excited, his lips moving faster, his hands fluttering. A flame licks up a branch. The trunk turns red like an ember in a dying fire, but Humboldt's words are like a secret breath blowing, and the red glows brighter.

The tree is suddenly alight. The flames entwine it like a serpent. Within a moment, the tree is consumed, a charred hand twisted at the sky, smoke taken by the wind out over the forest. Humboldt stands before it, pleased with what he has wrought, a sick glimmer in his hating eyes. Wisdom is power. Power is wisdom. They are the same thing.

XII. The Hermit

HUMBOLDT HAS BEEN WANDERING the forest for several days when he almost trips on what he thinks is a log. The log grunts. Humboldt stops and looks at it.

The log is a leg. It is attached to a man, who staggers to his feet. The man is precisely as ragged as Humboldt: His beard is like unraveled rope, his clothing shredded, his thin knees protruding like dirty knuckles.

"Avast!" cries the man. "Ye disturb me slumber!"

Humboldt is silent. The two regard each other like twin crows, each suspecting the other is hiding a shiny thing.

"Avast, I say," says the man. "Ye scrub. Ye rusty windlass. Ye stained stanchion."

Humboldt thinks the man is crazy. The man peers suspiciously at him, and then starts back, a weird look of recognition in his gnarled face.

"Ah, ye be a fellow sailor, eh, mate? A fellow oar-heaver, aren't ye? A sail blower and a salt floater?" The man gathers his moustache in his fingers to show that he is smiling, then puffs his filthy cheeks and blows, making motions with his hands to indicate sails. He lurches about, grinning.

"Be silent, bones and bark," says Humboldt. "You jabber. Your words flap about."

The man staggers back as if a gale had surprised him amidships. "I thought ye were a man of the sea, by the look of ye."

"We're in a forest, babble-beard." Humboldt points to the trees around them. "Tree. Tree. Another tree. No water."

"Still, ye have a seaman's scars. The water's made its mark," says the man, squinting. "Come jig!" he cries, suddenly. "Come have a cloggy dance! The waves heave and crash and it makes me queasy to be standing still!"

The man clomps about flapping his arms, grunting and grinning. "Oh, the world is grand, and I shall sing it a song," he cries, and then launches into a tuneless shanty.

"Sing to the wild weird world,
    sing to the sad old sea!
To the hungry deep,
    I'll wail and I'll weep
For the sodden sailors before me.
Tomorrow was sunny,
    yesterday it will rain!

THE HERMIT

The sea it don't care
whether foul or fair,
it sloshes and washes all the same!
Our dear boat is sinking,
    and we're full to the brim!
Wisdom is joy
If you be king or a boy
Don't be mad, for none of us can swim!"

Humboldt stares at him. "Be still," he growls. "I'm no singing sailor. I'm a sorcerer."

The man stops dancing. He looks at Humboldt with one eye. "Ah. A sorcerer. Sorcerers don't float."

Humboldt thinks about hitting the man.

The man shuffles close. He glances over one shoulder and then the other, then cups his dirty hand to his mouth and whispers. Humboldt recoils from the man's breath.

"Have ye seen it, mate?"

"Seen what, gibber-garbage?"

"At night, do ye hear it rustle?"

"What rustles?"

"The Broom, sailor. The Broom is abroad."

Humboldt shoves the man away, growling. The man totters for a moment, blinking, and then shrugs, grinning. He wobbles off into the trees, working his arms like a rower, making the sound of waves.

XIII. The Knight

At last, Humboldt finds a road. He's not sure where it goes, but it must go somewhere, he thinks. And so he trudges along the cobbles, his shoes worn through, his toes gripping the stones.

The forest thins, and now the road meanders through pleasant green hills. A sheep or two graze in a field. A small part of Humboldt feels a glimmer of joy, out walking in the sun with just the right breeze blowing, not know-

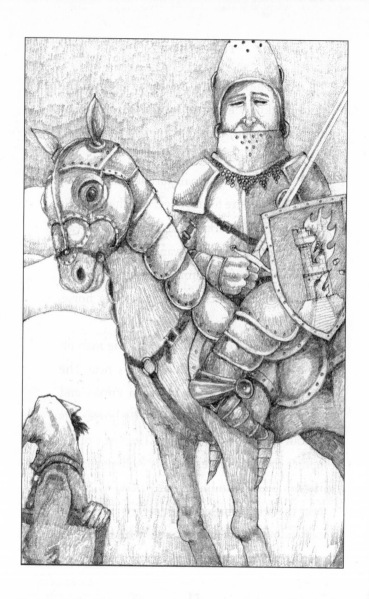

ing where he'll end up. When he lived in the castle he knew every stone and corner, every drip and shadow. Out here, there are surprises. He feels adventurous.

But that is only a small part of him. The rest surges with desire for revenge, and the desire is like a gobbling darkness in his brain. It eats every other thought that wanders by.

In the distance Humboldt sees a glint on the road. He squints. It is a man on a horse, approaching.

Humboldt keeps walking, and the man on the horse gets closer, until he is very near. The man is dressed in armour, which creaks and scrapes with the movement of the horse. His armour looks too big for him. The visor of his helmet covers his face, and it is evident that he has not seen Humboldt until now, when he jerks the reins, startled. They regard each other for a moment. The knight fusses with his sword until he manages to get it drawn.

The knight speaks and Humboldt cannot quite make out what he is saying through the metal. Something heroic sounding, as far as Humboldt can tell. Perhaps an introduction. He seems to be waiting for a response.

"I can't hear you," says Humboldt, pointing to his ear. The knight shifts in his saddle uncomfortably. He says something muffled, and then points at his own ear. Humboldt thinks he might have shrugged underneath his shoulder plates.

"Lift your visor," says Humboldt. The man leans a little to get closer, and it looks like he might lose his balance entirely. He mutters something unintelligible, manages to get himself properly in the saddle, and then flails about strangely. Humboldt realizes that the man is indeed trying to get his visor up.

Humboldt watches for a while until finally the visor tips. The man is gasping and sweaty. Humboldt waits for him to catch his breath.

"Lo, yonder peasant!" exclaims the knight, eventually. "I am entrusted with a quest. I shall not fail. For I am, as you can see, a knight of the holy order, a bearer of the sword of justice."

Humboldt does not say anything. The knight looks pleased with his proclamation. He remembers to hold his sword up, and then thinks of the next thing to say.

"Yonder peasant! Lo! The kingdom is like a thirsty man. It thirsts not for water, for a kingdom does not drink (although a king does, but that is irrelevant to my metaphor). No, the kingdom does not thirst for water, the kingdom thirsts for gold. Gold."

Humboldt darkens. The man continues. "Give me your gold. The King commands it. He is, as I say, thirsty for it, or rather the kingdom is. That is my quest."

Humboldt speaks. "I have no gold," he says. "Nor would I give it to you if I did."

The man frowns. "Don't be like that. This is

my task for the King."

"I have no fondness for the King. In fact, I am going to kill him."

"Pardon?"

"I am going to kill the King." As Humboldt says it, he realizes that is exactly what he is planning.

The knight looks around for a moment, trying to figure out what to do. He brightens. "Lo! I am the defender of the crown! I have sworn an oath to lay down my life in noble service!" He looks satisfied with that. The horse snorts.

"You are a chore boy, that is all," says Humboldt. "A chore boy for a king is still a chore boy."

The knight growls and suddenly Humboldt realizes that the horse is charging. He stumbles backward and trips on the hem of his cloak. He lands hard and scrambles desperately as the hooves clatter on the road and the sword flashes, swinging. Humboldt covers his face with his hands and shrieks whichever words come into his head.

The blow does not fall. Humboldt feels a sharp heat on his hands and hears a strange howling whoosh. Then, silence. He peers out from between his singed fingers.

The road is empty except for a pall of oily black smoke. The cobblestones are smeared with soot. A small bush is burning nearby.

Humboldt stands, flabbergasted. He picks up the Book, and walks on, looking behind him.

Half an hour later he finds the helmet lying by the road. He picks it up and wipes off the ashes. It is still a little warm. He puts it on, grinning.

XIV. The City

I CAN MAKE GOLD," says Humboldt. He is standing at the gates to the Imperial City.

The guards look at each other. "He can make gold, he says," says one, pushing his helmet off his brow. The other, leaning on his axe, strokes his moustache.

"Out of what? That's the question." They look back at Humboldt.

"One guy came round, said he could make gold. Turned out he could only make it out of rhinoceros horn dust and a particular flower juice from some mountain in what-have-you or wherever. Rare ingredients, you see. No good."

"Another guy, he could only make it out of rubies. The equation didn't work out, if you know what I'm saying. Rubies more expensive than gold."

"Out of what. That's the question."

Humboldt grins. "Out of anything. Toads. Trees. Guards. Myself, if you like."

"Well, then, the King will want to see you," says the guard with the helmet. He steps aside and waves up at the battlements. There is the rattle of great chains as the gates creak open.

Humboldt politely bids them goodbye and walks into the city.

It is wretched. Garbage is piled everywhere, and people search amongst the muck for unthinkable things, calling to each other in hoarse voices. Beggars in rags more tattered than Humboldt's jostle and brag at each other.

Somebody to Humboldt's right is being killed with a piece of old chicken, and to his left, somebody else is wailing incoherently and tearing at his hair. The roofs and gables are festooned with filthy urchins, who are pulling up the shingles and hurling them down at the people of the heaps.

The fetid ground slopes upward, and beyond the stench Humboldt can see the stairs to the second gate. Above that he can see the third and the fourth, each gate higher than the last, until he cannot see farther in the smog of the garbage fires. At the distant top, apparently, is the King.

Humboldt shoves his way through the crowd, dirty hands pulling at his clothing and at his Book. He elbows and kicks and grimaces as he goes, and is glad for his helmet when a shingle breaks on his head. The masses broil and seethe around him, but he makes it to the stairs.

He is used to stairs. He clambers rapidly out of the mire, the urchins jeering at him because they cannot go where he is going. The next guards have trouble hearing him over the shouting, but soon he is through.

The next layer of the city is not much better. Humboldt is instantly surrounded by barking people, bumping and pushing. They wave things at him, shoes and carpets and house-robes and trinkets, yowling prices and special deals and must-go sales. Humboldt cannot budge in the throng, until he pulls his pockets out to show that they are empty. Immediately he is deserted, the pack of vendors swirling away, trying to sell things to each other.

The third layer is a cacophony. Everywhere musicians prance, strumming and blowing, singing and weeping. Poets declaim from windows at the top of their lungs, and actors deliver soliloquies at high speed, pausing occasionally to bow to one another with elaborate flourishes. Two painters stab at each other with brush ends, one trying to paint a forest nymph scene and the other a famous battle on the same piece of crumbling wall. A man in spectacles shouts at Humboldt: "Chapter 15! What happens in Chapter 15?" and then staggers off, whimpering.

The fourth layer is finally quiet. Humboldt picks his way over sprawled and slumbering philosophers. An aged fellow is attempting to describe his theory on the ultimate arbitrariness of signification, and the consequent nature of consciousness, but he keeps parenthesizing, frequently in German, and finally loses his train of thought entirely and nods off, his toes twitching slightly.

Humboldt is beleaguered in the fifth layer. At first he thinks it will be easy to pass through, because everything is organized and the people are dressed in efficient outfits, but each one he asks for directions gives him a form to fill out and then a line to stand in. He tries shouting but nobody listens. Finally he makes a run for it, forms fluttering behind him, and after a while he discovers the right street.

The sixth is easier to slip through. Everybody is standing at attention or shouting orders or marching about. The air is filled with clangs and tromping, but nobody seems to notice Humboldt in the midst of their complicated maneuvers.

And finally he stands before the open gate to the seventh level of the city.

XV. The Usurper

THE THRONE ROOM is filled with gold. Teetering piles of coins point at the roof like stalagmites in a cave. Chests overflow, spilling onto the flagstones; heavy bags are stacked in ponderous heaps. The walls are lined with shelves, and the shelves with glittering cups, trophies, rings, necklaces, dismantled icons, and dental fillings.

In the centre of the room is a great iron cauldron, full of melted gold, glowing with

heat. Three men in black, their faces calloused with burns, stand hunched around it. One stirs with a great iron ladle, another skims the impurities, and the third gathers more gold for the pot.

Behind the cauldron is a frightening thing. It is a gigantic statue of the King, made of gold, reaching almost to the ceiling. The statue is a disturbing likeness except that it is unfinished: it has no arms and its head is only half-poured. Its bottom teeth and beard are done, but above is empty air. The three men in black are making a golden king.

It is difficult to see through the glare. Humboldt cannot spot the King himself. On the far wall, between the statue's legs, is a door.

There is a bang as the door is flung open. There stands the King. Behind him is what appears to be his bedroom.

The cauldron three turn and bow. The King grunts and spits. He looks at the statue with a baleful glare, and then back at the blackened bowers.

"Faster," he growls.

He looks around at the piles of gold. "More. More gold."

The silent men bow even deeper.

Over their backs the King notices Humboldt.

"Who?" says the King, his jaw clenched.

"Sorcerer," says Humboldt.

The King's beard catches fire like dry grass. He swats at it, his cruel eyes wide, but suddenly his robes too are aflame. He spins in place, flailing, as Humboldt murmurs.

Humboldt's finger twitches and the King is aloft, hurtling through the air, trailing smoke in black spirals. He twists and thrashes in mid-air, grimly silent, and then evaporates in a ball of fire that fills the room with a ghastly light, playing on the backs of the cauldron men, the coins fusing into golden pillars like gnarled trees. Humboldt's shadow burns into the wall, a giant spectral mural of murder.

The fire extinguishes with a lingering howl and the King is no more. A snowfall of ash gently falls.

The cauldron men look at Humboldt. Humboldt looks back.

"King," he says. "Sorcerer King."

The men bow.

XVI. The Coronation

THE PEOPLE OF THE SEVEN LEVELS are gathered. The crowning of the Sorcerer King Humboldt the First is a lavish affair.

The people of the heaps are there, as well as the sellers, the artists, the professors, the bureaucrats, and the army. They have found themselves in formation, bowing low, unable to prevent themselves. Their new lord is impressive to them.

They gasp in unison when the fireworks

begin. Over their heads, the entire sky turns bright with flame as if the world had been engulfed in the belly of a dragon. The roar is deafening. It forms into words.

"Subjects: You are now ruled by His Highness Humboldt the First, Sorcerer King. I am mighty and I am merciless. Nevertheless, you are lucky, for I am also wise. What I order is good for you. Do not seek to understand. Simply obey.

"These are your chores."

The people hear the list and do as they are told.

XVII. The Tyrant

THE SORCERER KING can't sleep. He lies amongst tousled sheets in the imperial bed. The drapes have been pulled tight by servants, but somehow the moon leaks in, illuminating the flagstones like a pale liquid spilled on the floor and running along the cracks. On the bedside table sits a forlorn mushroom, shriveled and black.

Humboldt stares at the ceiling. Under his head is the Book, but the rest of his body is

sprawled all gangly. His mind is wandering: For a moment he ponders the relationship of mercury to dragons, promising himself to research it in the morning, and then he thinks about toads and lightning. He wonders if he could possibly succeed where his master failed. He is wondering if he could make gold. He has melted down the unfinished statue of the King to make a new one of himself, but he has run out of gold, and the knights say they cannot find any more, even when they are tortured.

He hears a rustle in the shadows and he sits up, the Book in his arms. He peers around him. Nothing but darkness. He blinks and the candles are alight, but there is nothing but the heavy drapes and the bedposts flickering in the glow.

Humboldt thinks he has been deceived by the night, that there was no rustle. The candles extinguish as he lies back down.

Another rustle, right next to him. A soft

whisper in his ear. "Humboldt," it says. "One day. . . ."

Humboldt is out of bed and the candles are ablaze. There is nothing in the room. On the sheet, Humboldt sees a piece of straw. He will not sleep again.

XVIII.
The Conflagration

A LL BROOMS MUST BE BURNT."

The assembled court—generals, ministers, philosophers, official artists, wealthy merchants, and gang leaders—bow with assent. Humboldt sits on his throne above them. He has the Book on his lap and a toad on the book, which he strokes. His face is haggard from perpetual waking. His eyes are dark. When he twitches his eyebrow the court shudders.

"All cleaning implements whatsoever. It is my decree that there will be bonfires in every square. Those who withhold their brooms will be added to the fire. Not a single broom shall remain in this kingdom. Burn."

The orders are posted, the army deployed. The streets are filled with the rough clank of boots and gauntletted fists pounding on doors. Brooms are dragged from the hands of startled janitors, grandmothers, apprentices. Broom closets are kicked open and their contents thrown into the back of iron carts, which rumble through the city according to an efficient choreography designed by the bureaucrats. Soon the squares are piled high with brooms, mops, dusters, whisks, toilet scrubs, chimney sweeps, kitchen swabs, barbecue marinators, brushes for painting or teeth, even rags, dishcloths, towels, back scratchers, nose blowers, table wipers, rubber gloves—anything remotely connected with cleaning.

Then the bonfires are lit, and the city glimmers with the eradication of the broomish kind.

The army marches out the lower gates, the seven regiments each taking one of the seven roads that extend from the imperial city like spokes from a flaming hub. Their carts rattle behind them and their banners flutter in the drifting smoke.

Soon the entire kingdom is filled with fire. And soon the entire kingdom is filthy, since nobody can sweep up the falling ash and the mud dragged in by the soldiers' boots.

But still, Humboldt hears the sinister rustle in his bedroom at night.

"Humboldt," it whispers. "One day. . . ."

"Humboldt," it whispers. "One day soon. . . ."

"Humboldt," it whispers. "Tomorrow."

XIX. The Broom

ALL NIGHT HUMBOLDT HEARS strange noises outside his door. He cowers in his bed, the sheets wrapped around him like a funeral shroud. He is delirious with lack of sleep, his eyes hollow. The room warps and wobbles in his vision.

He doesn't want to be Sorcerer King any more. He doesn't want anything to do with any of it. He wishes he was still just doing his chores, back in the Sorcerer's castle, nothing

but an apprentice. He wishes he had never seen the Book.

He has pored over it endlessly, trying to determine a way to silence the Broom. But the Book has nothing to say. On the inside back cover, Humboldt finds words he has never seen before. They are scrawled in the Sorcerer's hand:

"Humboldt, I do forgive you. You could not help it. It was my fault that I left the key, and worse, that I did not teach you better. In the end it may have been impossible to change you, as indeed it is impossible to change anything truly once it has awakened. Wisdom is sorrow. I now accept that the Broom cannot be defeated. I only hope it will be satisfied with me."

Humboldt hurls the Book across the room, and it lands heavily. He lurches out of bed and grabs a lantern, then stands teetering over the crumpled pages on the floor. He feels himself unscrewing the lid and pouring the oil onto the

Book, then tossing the empty thing aside. He has a candle flickering in his hand. He is kneeling.

He feels a prickle on the back of his neck. He turns, and there, against the door, leans the Broom.

Humboldt drops the candle, which is extinguished as it falls. The Book lies sodden.

Words tumble from Humboldt's mouth, words of the greatest power he can muster. He names things of the deeps and things of the black sky beyond the clouds. He utters the forgotten syllables of the first words spoken when the universe was darkness without age. His arms rise, trembling.

Holy fire streams from his throat. He is a dragon. The molten centre of the earth and the ember heart of the sun envelop the Broom, flowing around it like an apocalyptic wind. And yet the Broom is unscorched.

Through the warped air Humboldt notices

at the last moment that the door behind the Broom is strained and bulging, just as the wood disintegrates in the flames. And Humboldt knows what the Broom has done.

Ten thousand tons of water burst through the door frame. The Broom has filled the castle while Humboldt cowered.

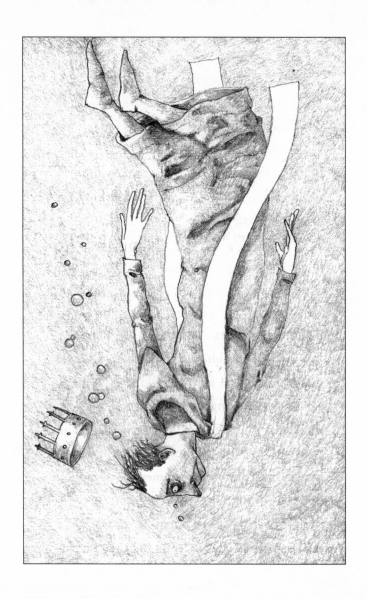

XX. The Flood

THE FLAMES EXTINGUISH instantly, and Humboldt hears the hiss as the water hits him like the fist of a god. He is hurled against the ceiling and then sucked under, thrashing, gulping, the flood in a tumult of twisting currents, spinning Humboldt, tossing him, tearing him without mercy. All around him is foam and flow.

The water reaches down his throat like a ghoulish thing. His lungs fill, and then there is

a muffled rending as the walls explode.
Humboldt finds himself thrust to the surface,
tossed on the arching wave, crashing down.
The city is engulfed, buildings smashing like
ant bones under boots. People swirl past, gulping and shrieking. Chimneys crumble, carts are
tossed, swords and harps and paper and garbage
are snatched into the whirling tide. The whole
collapsing architecture is like a ferocious foun-
tain overflowing.

And Humboldt is swept into the sea. On
all sides is water, salty like tears in Humboldt's
mouth. He gurgles, trying to speak, but a final
swell flows over his head, and he is pulled
under.

Underwater the cosmos slows and
Humboldt feels a dreadful peace. He sees his
arms moving and feels his lungs bulge in his
chest, but it no longer matters to him. A strange
gold light fills his mind, obliterating all his
memories. The water feels warm. He tries to

formulate his last thoughts, but he finds he knows no words. All that remains is the steady throb of an enormous heart which he doesn't think is his own. And then he doesn't even know what difference there might be if it is his heart or not: Humboldt's heart, or the heart of the world? He cannot remember who Humboldt is. He is about to die.

But then comes the voice of the Sorcerer.

HE WHO DROWNS
BE NOW UNDROWNED
WATER NOW UNPOUR
ALL THAT'S DONE BE NOW UNDONE
BROOM BE BROOM ONCE MORE

XXI. The World

Humboldt is sprawled on the dry castle floor. The Sorcerer stands above him, his eyebrows black, his face fierce.

Humboldt winces as he gathers his broken body and stands, hunched, before his master.

The Sorcerer points to the bucket.

Humboldt looks at it. He looks back at the Sorcerer. In the far corner rests the Broom, leaning.

Humboldt does not pick up the bucket. He walks silently past his master, down the hall.

He blinks into the sunlight through the open gates, and then limps into the forest, making rowing motions with his arms, smiling. The world is before him, golden sunlight on the green trees and fields. He finds himself singing.

"Sing to the wild weird world,
   sing to the sad old sea!
To the hungry deep,
I'll wail and I'll weep
For the sodden sailors before me.
Tomorrow was sunny,
   yesterday it will rain!
The sea it don't care
whether foul or fair,
it sloshes and washes all the same!
Our dear boat is sinking,
   and we're full to the brim!

THE WORLD

Wisdom is joy
If you be king or a boy
Don't be mad, for none of us can swim!"

THE END

THE END

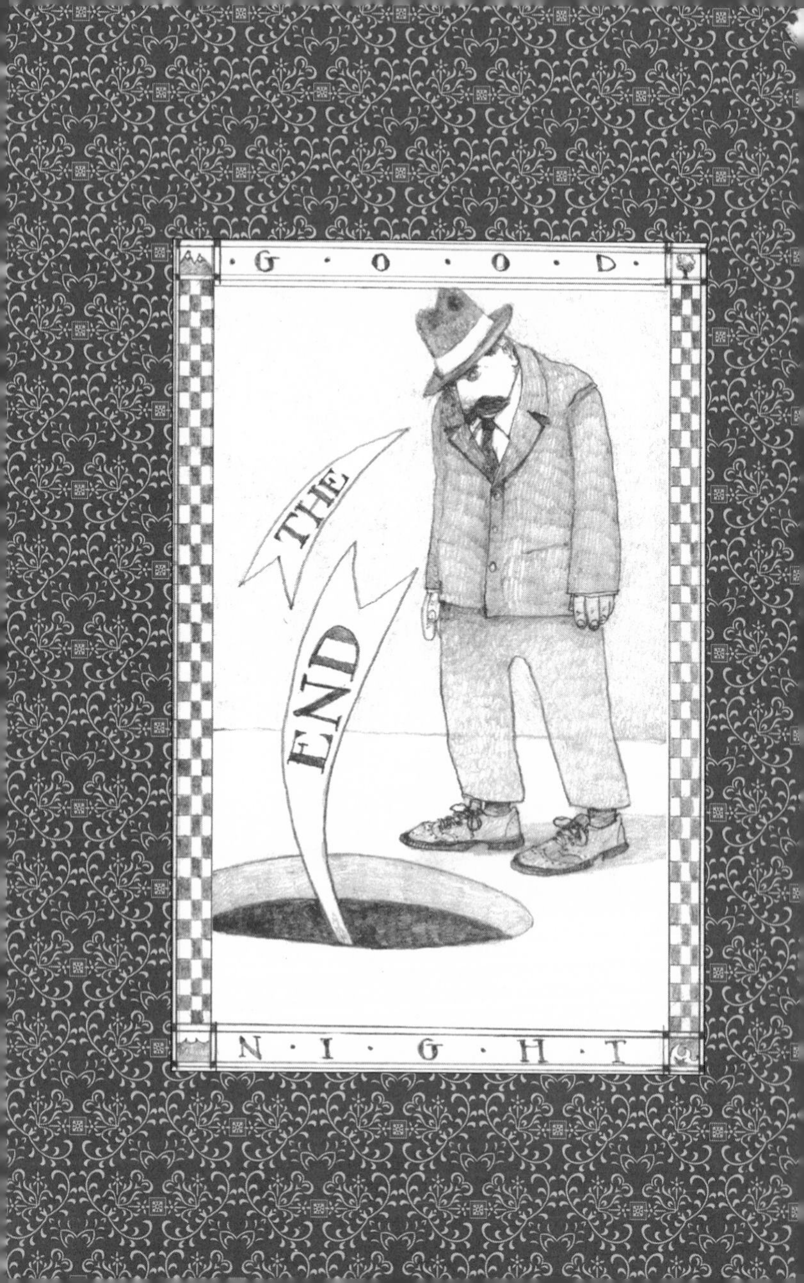
G·O·O·D
THE
END
N·I·G·H·T